For Luke & Alice —M.H.

To Bonnie, who puts up with it —J.S.

Manufactured in China by C&C Offset Printing Co. Ltd. Shenzhen,
Guangdong Province, in November 2015

Published by Little Bigfoot, an imprint of Sasquatch Books
20 19 18 17 16   9 8 7 6 5 4 3 2 1

Editors: Tegan Tigani and Christy Cox
Production editor: Em Gale
Design: Anna Goldstein

Back endsheet courtesy of the *Seattle Times*

Library of Congress Cataloging-in-Publication Data is available.

ISBN: 978-1-63217-003-3

Sasquatch Books
1904 Third Avenue, Suite 710
Seattle, WA 98101
(206) 467-4300
www.sasquatchbooks.com
custserv@sasquatchbooks.com

THE AUTHOR WISHES TO THANK:

Pat Patrick, Dan Raley, Harry Yoshimura, Remo Borracchini, Museum of
History and Industry (MOHAI), Rainier Valley Historical Society, Seattle
Public Library, Northwest African American Museum (NWAAM), Pete Stolpe,
Elisha Cooper, Tegan Tigani, Carolyn Holtzen, and Dave Eskenazi

A TICKET TO

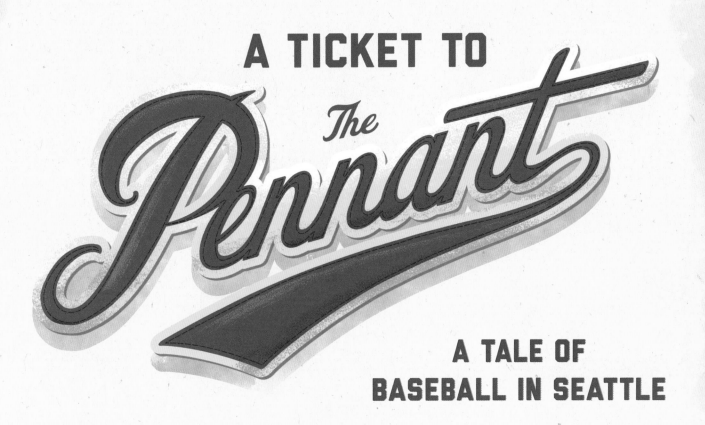

The Pennant

A TALE OF BASEBALL IN SEATTLE

Mark Holtzen

Illustrated by
John Skewes

little bigfoot
an imprint of sasquatch books
seattle, wa

SEATTLE RAINIER
BASEBALL CLUB
★ GAME 4 ★
PACIFIC COAST LEAGUE FINALS
2.00 P.M.
SATURDAY SEPT. 10, 1955
EST. PR. $1.08   TOTAL $1.25
FED. TAX .11
CITY TAX .06
RAINCHECK – In event 4½ innings of game are not
played, this coupon good for any regular game this
season. Exchange at Box Office.
FRED HUTCHINSON
MANAGER

RIGHT GRAND STAND
SEC 8
ROW 8
SEAT 3

Huey had his glove, his lucky shirt, and his cap. He was all ready for the game. Now he just needed his Rainiers to win. And he needed his ticket.

Today was the deciding game of the series between the Seattle Rainiers and the Los Angeles Angels, but Huey couldn't find his ticket. He had searched everywhere. Where could it be?

He had it yesterday when he went shopping with his mother. He would have to retrace his steps on the way to the stadium.

The game started in twenty minutes!

He ran out of the house. His next-door neighbor sat listening to the radio.

"Mr. Barnett, have you seen my ticket?" Huey asked.

"Nope. You lost it?" Huey nodded his head yes. "Well, you're welcome to listen on the porch with us, Huey."

Announcer Leo Lassen's nasal voice came over the radio:

"The Rainiers and Angels are here at Sicks' Stadium in Seattle, baseball fans. The Suds and Halos have taken batting practice. Pitchers are warming up. It's been a tight race for the pennant."

Lassen continued to warm up the fans: "*Stephens is on the hot corner; Balcena is patrolling center. Mount Rainier is a big ice cream cone over Franklin High tonight, folks.*"

"Lemonade, Huey?" Mrs. Barnett asked. Their porch was tempting.

"No thanks, Mr. and Mrs. Barnett. I gotta find my ticket."

Huey ran down Dearborn to Rainier Avenue and turned left. Bus number seven rolled by. As he scanned the ground for his ticket, the smell of Italian cooking almost distracted him. Mmm—meatballs or ravioli?

Huey thought he could hear the murmur of the stadium twelve blocks away.

Near the I-90 Bridge, he heard Leo from a car radio:

"Kretlow's off to a shaky start. Two Angels aboard."

Huey's gut tightened. After two more blocks, he neared
Borracchini's Bakery, where he and his mother had
stopped yesterday for bread. Maybe he left his ticket there.

"Hi, Huey. Can you fetch me the tomatoes from the truck? Remo is more interested in the game," said Mrs. Borracchini, the baker's wife, rolling her eyes. "Like everyone else."

Huey groaned. He needed to find that ticket, but he wanted to be a good neighbor. "Sure, Mrs. B.," he said and dashed outside.

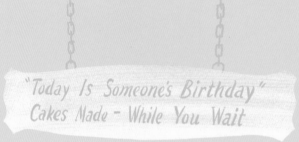

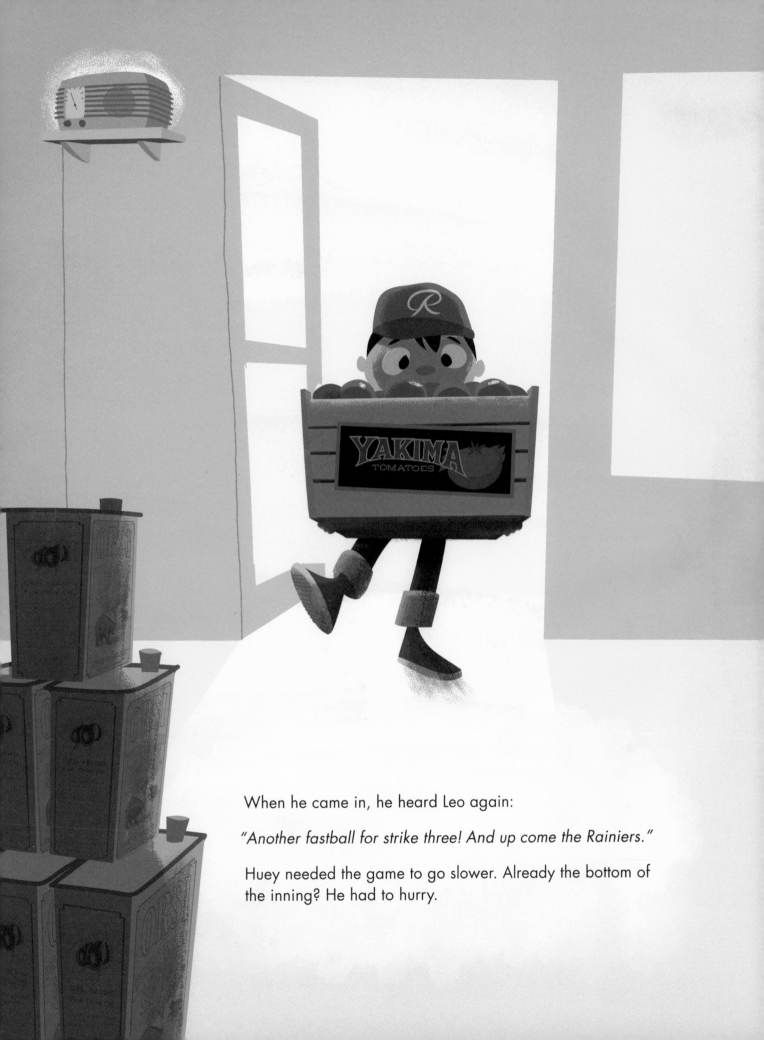

When he came in, he heard Leo again:

"Another fastball for strike three! And up come the Rainiers."

Huey needed the game to go slower. Already the bottom of the inning? He had to hurry.

"Did you find a ticket lying around, Mrs. Borracchini? I lost mine."

"Oh goodness no, Huey. I'm so sorry. Good luck! Thank you for your help."

Huey paused in the doorway to listen.

"Hutch has all right-handers in the lineup tonight to face Joe Hatten, the Halos' southpaw. Basgall steps up . . . "

"Anytime, Mrs. B"—and Huey raced down Rainier Avenue.

The street was quiet.

Huey overheard Leo's voice through the window of an apartment building:

"Basgall took third on a wild pitch after his double to left! Now Righetti's up. You can't say Righetti's had a hot bat this year, but let's see if he can bring Basgall home . . . "

Huey sprinted to Mutual Fish next. Had he left the ticket near the crab tank yesterday while his mother chose the trout? The bell over the door rang as he zipped in.

The crowd at the stadium, just two blocks away, roared. It was so loud Huey could hear it even after the door closed.

"Why aren't you at the game, Huey?" asked Mr. Yoshimura.
"And how was the fish last night?"

"It was good, thanks," Huey said. "But I can't find my ticket.
Have you seen it?"

From behind the counter, Lassen's voice echoed from the shop radio:

"Righetti punches a single to left. Basgall comes across the plate. Rainiers score!"

Mr. Yoshimura hadn't seen the ticket and was closing up early. The rest of the fishmongers were already at the game.

After a quick good-bye, Huey ran on toward the stadium.

A block away he realized he had forgotten his glove at the fish store and had to race back to get it.

Huey burst onto the street. He could see Mount Rainier on the horizon. Off to the left loomed Sicks' Stadium, tall and gleaming against the green hills of the Mount Baker neighborhood.

The stands came into view. Cars filled the parking lot, and fans filled the wooden bleachers. Cheapskate Hill outside left field—where those who didn't or couldn't pay watched the game from the Vacca family farm—was full too.

GAME 4
PCL CHAMPIONSHIP
SATURDAY SEPT. 10

Huey zoomed past the house where Kenneth from his baseball team lived. He saw The Barrel burger joint. It would be packed after the game with Rainiers fans and maybe even some players.

A radio sat on a stack of crates at Pre's Garden Patch. A small crowd gathered around.

"Balcena is up to bat. The Filipino Flychaser looks good tonight, folks. They could use his speed on the bases."

Balcena was Huey's favorite—a great hitter and fast too. Huey even got his autograph at The Barrel once. But how could it already be the bottom of the second?

Huey ran faster. He veered into a group standing along the wall in the parking lot. He saw his classmate Jane, who sometimes got in if she returned a ball to the ballpark.

"What are you doin' out here, Huey?" Jane hollered.

"I can't find my ticket," Huey said.

Jane smacked her forehead. "Unless someone hits a ball over this fence, we're not seein' nuthin'."

It was the top of the third. This was his last place to find the ticket!

He rushed to Mr. Prontera's shop. Huey saw the quickly scrawled sign: "Closed for the game." Now what was he going to do?

A cheer went up. Was another Angels batter out? Did Balcena just make a great play in center field? He had to know.

Huey grabbed his hat and swatted it against his thigh in frustration.

He stretched out his hands and yelled at the sky, **"WHERE IS MY TICKET?"**

He looked down. There was his ticket,
fluttering to the ground. It landed at his feet.

"Well, I'll be," he said.

Now he remembered he had put it in his hat the day before for safekeeping. Huey picked the ticket up and ran across the street to the front gates. The crowd cheered.

"Little late, aren't ya?" the ticket taker said. "Ya know they're playing for the pennant today, right, kid?" Huey ran, bumping through the crowd.

There they were. His Rainiers.

Huey moved through the aisles to the left-field bleachers. Another cheer went up. Righetti, the infielder, ran toward first. Basgall was already crossing home plate.

"Rainiers are up three to nothing in the bottom of the fourth!"

A nearby hot dog hustler hollered, "Hot dogs, getcher hot dogs!" A woman blew a piercing whistle. Huey loved it all.

The manager, Hutch, watched from the steps looking over the field. Balcena stood in the dugout. Huey's friend Pat, the batboy, waved.

"Huey, hello!" Huey's teacher, Mrs. Severson, called from one row down. "Great game, isn't it? Here, we have an extra seat cushion."

He thanked her and sat down. "You're late," his teammate Kenneth said, handing Huey a bag of peanuts.

Huey took a deep breath. He'd made it, and the Rainiers were ahead. But he knew better than to get too relaxed.

Anything can happen in baseball.

They filled out their scorecard and ate a hot dog through the fifth, shelled peanuts in the sixth, then sang "Take Me Out to the Ball Game" and stretched during the seventh. It was still three to zero, Rainiers. At the top of the eighth, the crack of a bat put them on the edge of their seats.

"It's a single! Looks like trouble, folks," announced Leo.

Sometimes Huey wished Leo wasn't so honest.

Huey, along with the rest of the crowd, cringed at yet another base hit. The Angels scored. It was 3–1. Hutch called for another pitcher—the dependable Bill Kennedy.

But the ninth inning started off no better.

"Fireman Bill walked him," Leo said. *"The tying run's at the plate. This does not look good, Rainiers fans."*

With one man on base, Kennedy struck out the next batter; then he struck out another. Two outs. The Rainiers could still win. Or they could still lose.

"Not a fingernail left in the stadium, folks."

Kennedy threw the pitch. A sharp grounder to third. Zernia, the third baseman, dove for the ball and threw to Glynn at first, but—oh no! The ball bounced into the dirt . . .

. . . but Glynn stretched and dug the ball out of the dirt and into his glove. The final out!

Huey and the rest of the crowd leapt from their seats. Everyone threw cushions high into the air until they fell like snow from the sky. Huey saw Mr. Borrachini, the baker, cheering; Mr. Yoshimura nearby backslapping a fellow fishmonger; and the barber, Mr. Prontera, shaking hands with Mrs. Severson.

From the radio, Leo yelled, *"Seattle has won the pennant!"*

AUTHOR'S NOTES:

- In 1950s Seattle, baseball was the only game in town. Men's and women's amateur teams played all over the region, but the heart of the city belonged to the Seattle Rainiers. The team battled rivals like the Oakland Oaks, the San Francisco Seals, and the Portland Beavers. These clubs were part of the Pacific Coast League (PCL)—a high-level minor league a notch below the majors. Future major leaguers Ted Williams and Joe DiMaggio got their start in the PCL. The Seattle Rainiers were dominant in that era, winning five championships.

  Today, Seattle has a Major League Baseball (MLB) team, the Seattle Mariners, as well as the Tacoma Rainiers, which are the Mariners' Triple-A farm team.

- When beer baron Emil Sick bought the Seattle PCL team in 1937, he changed their name from the Indians to the Rainiers and built a new stadium on McClellan and Rainier Avenue in diverse Rainier Valley. Sicks' Stadium was the pride of the Pacific Coast League, with a capacity near twelve thousand.

- Leo Lassen, "The Great Gabbo," was "The Voice" of Seattle baseball from 1931 until 1960. TV broadcasts began in 1949 but people watching still kept the radio on to hear Leo.

- Outfielder Bobby Balcena was the first player of Filipino descent to play professionally in the United States. He was fast, friendly, and a favorite of kids. He gave Pat Patrick, the bat boy, his Wilson glove at the end of the '56 season.

- Fred Hutchinson was signed to the Rainiers out of Franklin High School in South Seattle, after the 1937 high school baseball season. "Hutch" went on to be a respected major league player and manager for twenty-two years—ten as a player and twelve as a manager. He was diagnosed with cancer at age forty-four. His brother, Dr. William Hutchinson, named Seattle's Fred Hutchinson Cancer Research Center to honor his memory. The Hutch Award, awarded annually since 1965, is given to a major league player who shows "honor, courage, and dedication."

- Dewey Soriano, the general manager of the Rainiers, joined the team in 1939. In 1955 he recruited Hutch to manage, but he had played ball with Fred since they were boys in the Rainier Valley.

- Mutual Fish and Borracchini's Bakery have been in business since before 1955. Mutual Fish was at a Jackson Street location then, but the author relocated it to its current Rainier Avenue address. This, as well as other geographical liberties, have been taken for the purpose of telling the story.

GET MORE OUT OF THIS BOOK

GROUP DISCUSSION

- Ask readers, "Have you ever misplaced something? How did you feel?"

- Discuss why Huey wanted "to be a good neighbor." Discuss what that expression means or could mean in various cultures.

- Discuss how the setting and characters are changing, including key details as evidenced by the illustrations and text.

GROUP ACTIVITIES

- Ask readers to create a "Baseball Language" poster to collect phrases and expressions in the story that may seem like baseball lingo. Encourage readers to point out sentences and ask questions about where they think baseball lingo may be used in the story.

- Ask readers to describe the overall structure of the story, including how the beginning is an introduction, the middle develops details, and the ending concludes the action. Have readers retell the story by recounting key details in complete sentences and answering the question, "What is the central message of the story?"

INDEPENDENT ACTIVITIES

- Compare the illustrations in the book to real pictures of streets and landmarks in Seattle through media searches on the Internet.

- Write about how Huey's character and the adults' experiences in the story might have been the same or different.

- Do a research project on the name Rainier, noting the team name, street name, and name of the mountain mentioned in the story.

TEACHER'S GUIDE: The above discussion questions and activities are from our teacher's guide, which is aligned with the Common Core State Standards for English Language Arts that can be adapted to Grades K–5. For the complete guide and a list of the exact standards it aligns with, visit our website: SasquatchBooks.com.

Rainiers Beat Angels

The Seattle Sunday Times

Sports

26

SUNDAY, SEPTEMBER 11, 1955.

VIEWS OF SPORT
By RED SMITH

Archie Moore, Actor, Plays Many Parts

NORTH ADAMS, Mass., Sept. 10.—Ever since John L. Sullivan toured in "Honest Hearts and Willing Hands," the American theater has offered refuge to fist fighters of diminishing skill. Archie Moore, the light-heavyweight champion who seeks to be

Huskies Lose Season; Led...

Twisted Leg Halts Back; Scrimmage Toll Hits 5

By GEORGE M. VARNELL

Bobby Dunn, senior halfback, was lost for the season with a twisted right leg and four other